BODIES

Written by Jan Ellen

Illustrated by Fizza Ahmed

Rudling House Publishing Limited,
Kemp House, 152 City Road, London EC1V 2NX

Illustrated by Fizza Ahmed
Project Managed by Rahat Parveen

Published in the UK in 2015 by Rudling House.
A CIP catalogue record for this book is available
from the British Library.

ISBN 978-1-910957-01-1

Printed and bound by Interak, Poland

www.rudlinghouse.com

Foreword

We drew letters out of a hat (mine, pink.) 6 or 7 each. Determined to write short, pithy pieces about bodies. But did they? No. I did mine (smug) and then did all the others too. Hooked.

Thanks Rose Marie, Kate and Polly - for inspiration and leaving me to do all the work!

And so it began.

Showed some of them to my daughter, Clare. She'd got a book well on the way to publication. 'Show them to Karen (the publisher)' she says. Karen says, 'yes, go ahead, publish.' All a bit surreal. Me, publish a book?

'Needs to be illustrated,' says Clare. 'I'll get you an illustrator.' 'OK, an illustrator,' I think. Even more surreal. Then the illustrator is a Muslim woman. Bodies. Thought Muslims couldn't do faces. Plus, there's the odd Christian reference. Oh well.

But her stuff was good. Indian ink sketches, worked with the writing style. And she could do faces as long as there were no eyes.

'OK,' I thought. 'People looking in mirrors, out of windows, but no eyes. Let's go with it.'

And we did.

Fizza and Rahat, (Design Editor) are both Muslims, both studying to higher education levels but both expecting arranged marriages in the next year or so. I learnt a lot. What was it like to live as a Muslim in Britain? How did they feel about having their parents decide who they would marry? Both women were comfortable with their identities, committed to the Islamic faith but not fanatical. It was just a way of life. And the values didn't seem that much different from (proper) Christian values - look after people less fortunate than yourself, do no harm. I could identify with that. At Ramadan, in the hottest weather of that year, I heard about the regime. Admired and wondered why. Because I'm a practising atheist (philosophical agnostic.) I know the Bible well (A level Divinity.) Hence the odd Christian reference. I explained about heaven. They explained about heaven. Both seemed like good places to be even though I didn't believe either existed. And if they did ... well, I wouldn't be there. Where?

Thanks Fizza and Rahat - for your marvellous creativity and organization.

So 'Bodies' went on its way. No longer mine. It's all yours. Thank you for reading it.

ARROGANCE

I am such an incredibly handsome man.
I have big green captivating eyes.
My hair is thick, glossy and black.
Women flock to my side.
They swoon ceaselessly at my feet.
They cannot, just cannot, resist me.
My pert body is hard as steel,
My mind as sharp as a diamond.
I work out in my gym daily.
My penthouse apartment is uber-cool.
The London skyline views are magnificent
Like me.
I am called Narcissus.

and Answer

Belief or delusion?.
Helped by the green contact lenses.
Grecian 2000 black
Swiftly pass by on the other side.
Want to stamp on his feet.
Cannot resist vomiting.
Except for his prick (we've heard.)
No way in - or out.
A room full of mirrors.
Also full of mirrors.
He sees only himself.

We call him Nasty.

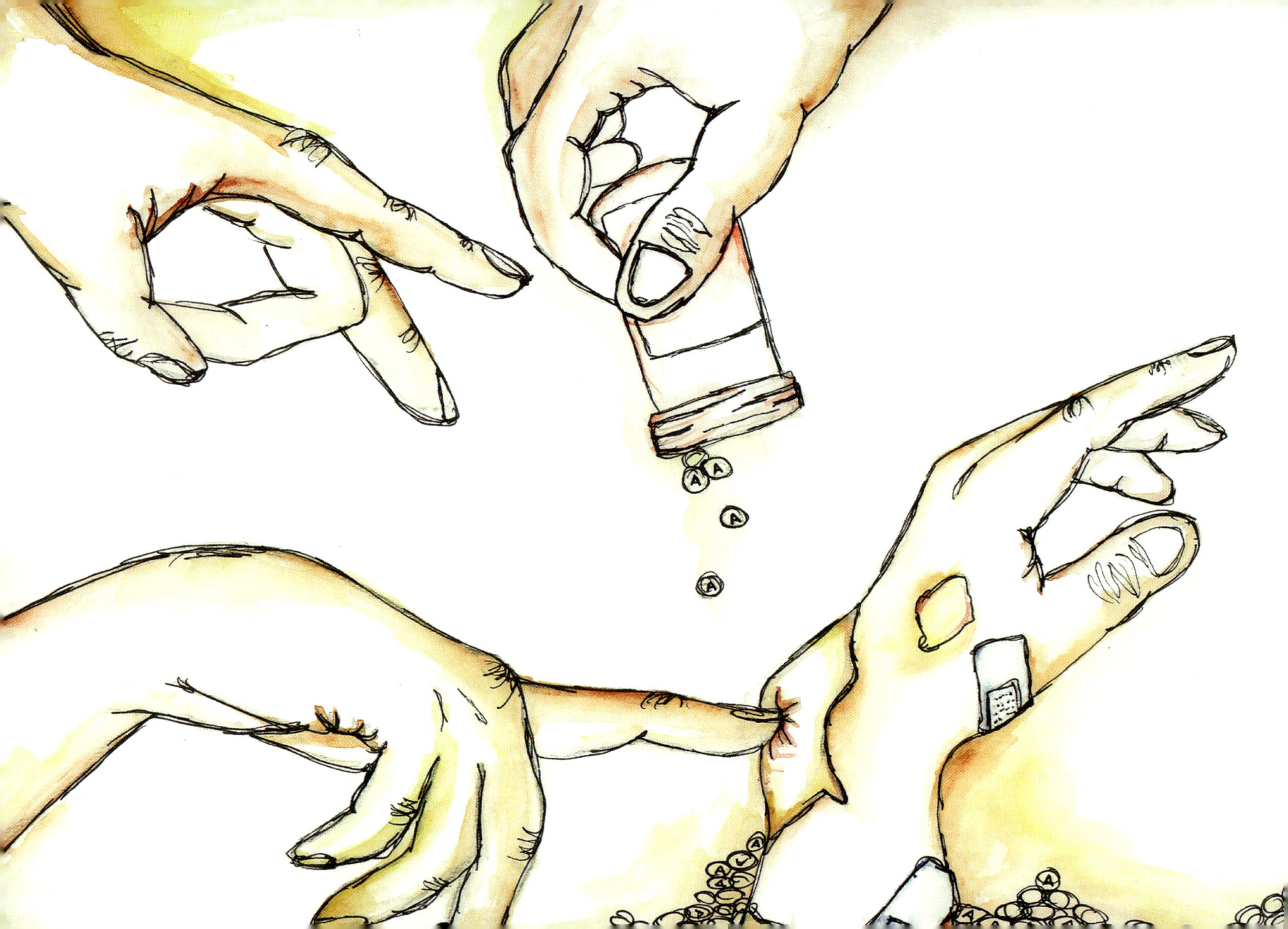

Boils

I thought he was intelligent. We'd had some good conversations - serious - his sense of humour was vestigial or, maybe, very dry. He was a regular visitor to the surgery. All the staff had to have their cuts covered each night. He seemed to have more than most and they didn't heal well. Tonight he was here again with his third boil this year. Worrying - could be diabetes. I needed to investigate this a bit more. A specimen of urine would be a start. He was reluctant.

'I've nothing to put it in.'

'We've run out of specimen pots. But a clean aspirin bottle would do,' I said.

He stayed and chatted a bit. Could there be world-wide agreement on climate control? We weren't optimistic.

The next night he turned up again - with boil - minus specimen.

'Where is it?' I wanted to know.

'Couldn't manage to take all the aspirin in time,' he said.

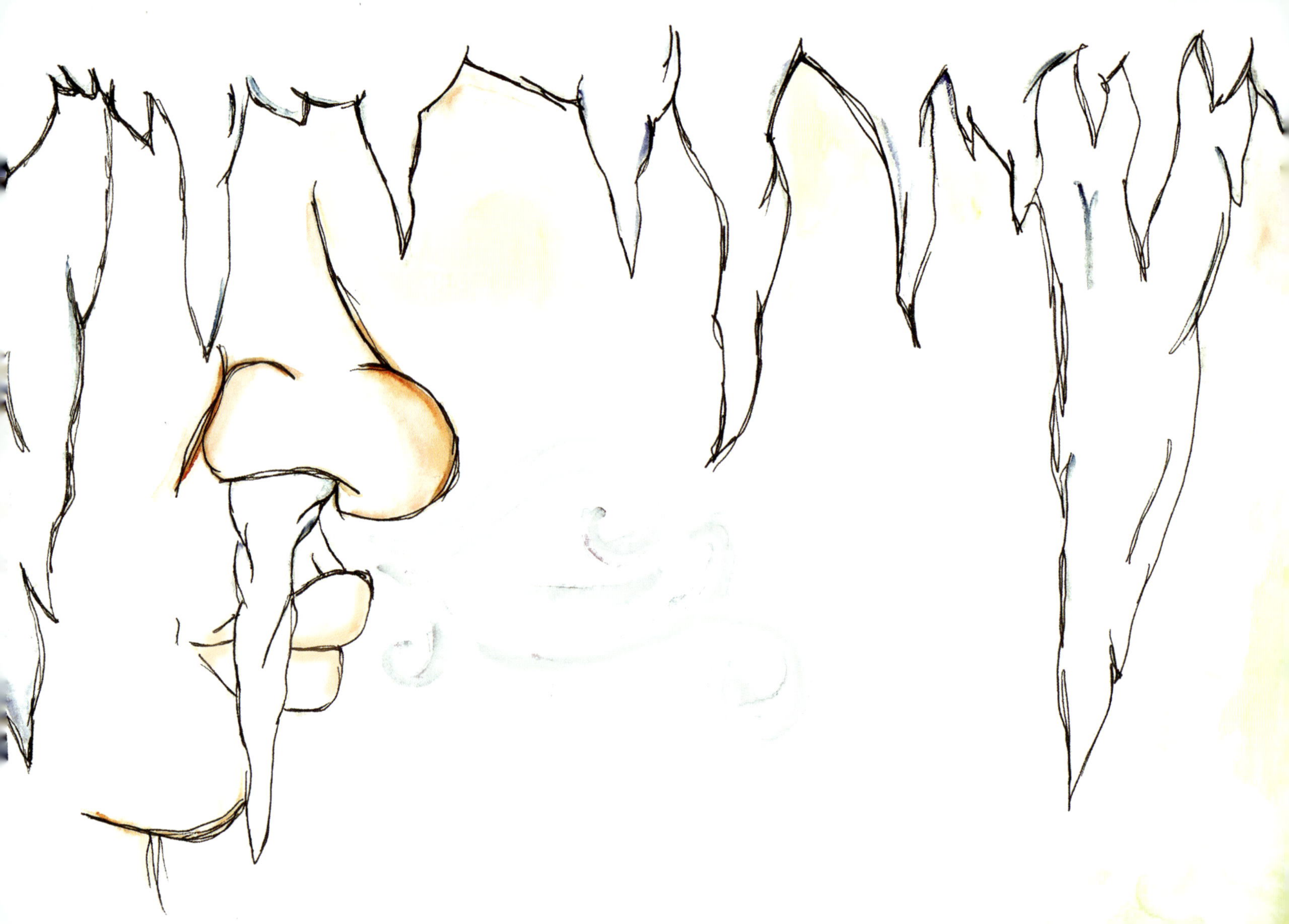

Cold

I was on the bus, on my way to the book group meeting. It was a nose-bitingly cold evening and I wanted to be home snug and warm, curled up beneath my duvet, just reading a book, not talking about one. But it was my turn to present so here I was. I had waited for the bus for a good ten minutes staring belligerently at the timetable that said they ran every six to eight minutes, wanting to sue for breach of promise, getting crosser by the second and shivering fit to shatter the glass in the shelter. But, at last, it had arrived, I'd climbed on, made an effort to be nice to the driver and taken a seat near the front. Now all that had to happen was a quick transit to my stop and a brisk walk to my destination.

But, no, that wasn't going to happen. We arrived at the stop up from the student village and a million students stood there waiting to board. I buried myself deeper into my sheepskin jacket, wriggled about to ease my buttocks in the two pairs of trousers I was wearing from necessity and flexed my now frost-bitten fingers and toes while I waited. The queue took so long to get on that more students joined it. I knew now I would never get to the book group - I could just see this line stretching out to eternity. I contemplated texting the hostess to warn her of my tardiness but couldn't face removing one glove.

Then the seat in front of me bounced a bit and I looked up from the misery of my coldness to confront a student wearing - you'll never guess - just a swimsuit! I looked away and swivelled my eyes back, sure it was only an illusion. Maybe my brain wanted sunshine making me hallucinate. No, it was still a swimsuit. Admittedly, it had those leg bits that competitive swimmers have to streamline their bodies but that was the only concession to cover it made; the lycra shoulder straps were thin, the back plunged daringly. In addition, there wasn't a goose pimple in sight! She turned her head and I noticed despairingly that there was no icicle hanging from the nostril, no frost glazing the eyelashes.

I was clearly a most inadequate person - no built-in central heating, no stamina, no will-power, no courage.

Oh to be a brave, resourceful, athletic student in a swimsuit!

I don't think so!

DEFINITELY NOT?

I won't have it. You cannot do this. Do not even try to persuade me. You are wrong. Space travel is impossible. You're in a fantasy world. You cannot be serious. Teleportation can't be done.

What do you mean you heard an alien calling to you, had a dream? Martin Luther King had a dream - look what happened to him. They lock people up who say things like that. Voices telling you how to do it indeed. Magic words! Abracadabra or something? What does that mean? What language was that? You don't know? Carry on not knowing is my advice.

You are sixty-four for god's sake. Too old! No-one becomes an astronaut at sixty-four.

Where do you have to be? The Paris metro? It won't work there. Underground. How can it? You've booked tickets? For us both? No! **No!**

NO!

What time?

I have to pack.

Eggshells

Do you remember that riddle? How did it go? Something like:

'In marble walls as white as milk
Encased in skin as soft as silk...'

I always think of that when I break an egg. They are so perfect aren't they? Actually quite hard to break. But crackable, as they have to be to let the life they have sustained out into the world. And when you boil an egg that skin inside is 'as soft as silk' but incredibly tough too. Sometimes it just won't give way.

I imagine them in the oviduct, shunting their way down, growing larger until they are ready to be 'born.'

Our pet hen, Esmeralda, used to 'deliver' in all sorts of strange places. Not for her the comfort of the hen house. Each day she would escape and lay her egg under a bush or in a clump of flowers - always a different place. So every day for us was an Easter egg hunt. Was she hiding them on purpose do you think? I got so I didn't want her eggs - they seemed so personally hers. But we ate them all the same. Heartless beasts us humans.

Of course this means that eggs in the hands of humans symbolise the end of life too. Whatever was beginning in there ended when we got hold of them.

What heartbreak for hens.

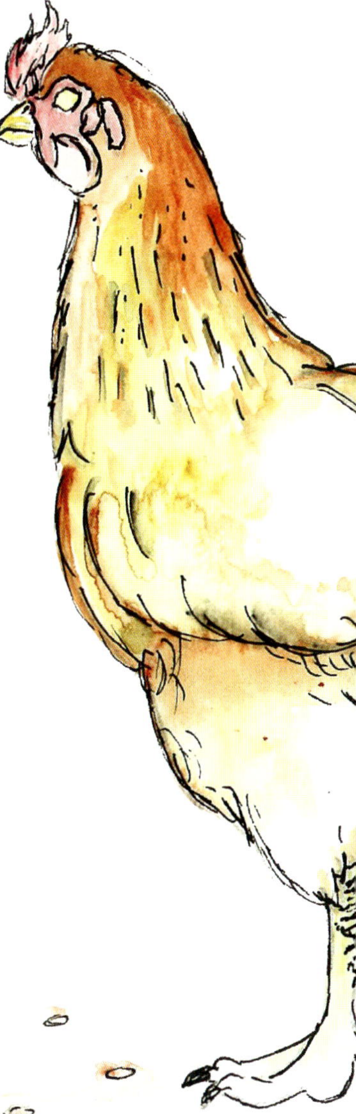

Funny

What's funny about the world? Why are people laughing? There's someone dying all the time - come to that we're all dying. As I see it, no hope of another life and, if this is all we've got, it's a pretty poor show on someone's part. (Is there even a 'someone'?)

Take yesterday, for instance.

I get up. Now that's an effort. Why would I do it? Well, I stink a bit and am fed up with the smell. So I take a shower. It's lukewarm. I hate lukewarm showers. But now I'm wet so I carry on. Soon it's a cold shower. I don't need no cold showers. Getting it up is hard enough! (Let alone doing anything with it.) Get out of there in a hurry, slip on the floor. Bang my head on the loo, bite my tongue, bash my ribs. Struggle to get up. Can't walk. Ankle already fatter than I'd like.

I've got one friend. So I phones him and, eventually he gets me down to the NHS Walk-In Centre. I suppose we have a bit of a laugh about that. Hobble-In Centre is what I call it!

I'm prepared for a long wait and am already getting myself psyched up to have a good old moan but we get greeted by a good looker of a nurse who peers down at my ankle and sends me straight off for an x-ray in a wheelchair. Walks with me and takes all my details along the way, stays, talks to the x-ray lass and tells me it's not broken but obviously badly damaged. We get back to the main bit and she straps it up, hoists me up on to a pair of crutches and watches me try them out. I'm crap! So she shows me how and I get better. We tackle stairs and I manage. A few painkillers in my pocket, I'm sent off, told to come back in a week if no better. Half-an-hour max. Can't believe it. Thought the NHS made you wait, matter of principle.

Get home and have a serious think.

Gutter

First thing Monday morning and I'm on the tube along with the rest of the world, standing close enough to at least two newspapers to read the small print. There's a good mix of people on here with me, like usual, range of colours, shapes, sizes. Feels healthy to me.

But the two newspapers I can see don't seem to think so. You can guess probably what they are but I'd better not name them just in case I write something I shouldn't. One headline effectively says 'they' are all taking 'our' jobs and another one, same newspaper, says they are skivers and only here because we're a soft touch. Seems to me you can't have it both ways. There's more of the same in the other one plus an article about muggings (all done by blacks, of course.) I am pretty angry by now.

An inspector gets on, looks at tickets, Oyster cards and the like. He's not satisfied with the student card of one Asian guy, says it doesn't look like him, implying it's been stolen. The guy is embarrassed but protests his innocence, quietly. The inspector isn't quiet and demands he pays full fare or the police will be called. They get off together at the next stop.

As soon as he leaves the mutterings start. I can hear those headlines all over again: 'our jobs,' 'skivers,' 'out for what they can get' etc. My slow-burning anger is fuelled, in much the same way, I guess, that the headlines have fuelled this situation. I cannot contain myself. I say loudly,

'That had nothing to do with the guy's ethnic origin.'

There is silence. Then some people look away, back to their books or gutter press. One or two smile at me, but mainly there's uproar, shouting at me to mind my own business, calling me paki-lover or equally horrible names. Fortunately, my stop is coming up soon, so I just stand there calmly, staring back, pleased to see at least one or two seem ashamed.

I get off. Someone walks along beside me and mutters a 'well done' in my ear.

'Needed saying,' he says.

'Why didn't you say it then?' I think, but keep cowardly silence, just like him.

HEAVEN

Oh, heaven was so boring. We stood around, all in white, wearing our crowns and doing that endless worship.

Actually, I'd only just made it in. 'Just about good enough,' was St Peter's grudging verdict, opening the gate just a slit. My last illness was debilitating, my body small and thin, so I managed to slip through. There were times when I wished I hadn't but, overall, supposed it was better to be eternally bored than eternally burned.

We were supposed to stand on the right hand side of the throne. There was competition for places right next to it. Jostling was difficult with those wings; none of us had been familiar with them, of course, and we took some time to get used to our new personal space. Angels started leaving their crowns beside the throne to keep their places. The rest of us either surreptitiously nudged them aside or didn't really care enough. I was in the latter group, preferring not to draw attention to myself. Sometimes God wanted a messenger and He picked at random someone close by. (Yes, sorry girls, He is definitely a man, witness the unmistakeable beard.) I never fancied a job like that, singing to shepherds or endlessly climbing up and down ladders. So, I put up with the boredom from the back of the host.

Somehow though, I'd managed to bring in a USB device. I kept it in the pocket of my gown. No idea what was on it. To while away the time, I watched the clouds that floated past constantly, looking for shapes like I used to when I was a child. One day, a USB port winked at me from a fold in a cloud. I followed it. Knew I wouldn't be missed. There were hosts and hosts of us. The cloud sailed gently along for a while then dipped into one of the many mansions behind the throne. I went in too. The room was huge and full of iclouds. What a result. I plugged in my device. Bliss, oh bliss! It was books, novels in the main, a good few thousand of them.

So, from then on, I was happy. I found my way quietly every day to the icloud mansion and read to my heart's content. The iclouds formed comfortable seats too. No-one seemed to notice, at first. Then, someone followed me. One of the disaffected crowd fortunately, so we took it in turns to read until we realised we could load the book on to one icloud, take out the device and plug it into another. Soon, other people followed and we formed a book group. That got too big and we formed a second. And so on. Then a writers' group formed and more books got added. Eternal literature followed.

And now heaven isn't so boring!

God
Confess
Sin
Pagan
Pray
Work
ethic
obey
Abstain

Ink

The Fraser Hegemony hums. Day after day it churns out paper, covered in words and images. The papers fly round the world and people read them. They cover more bits of paper and send them back. The Hegemony processes them and responds with yet more paper.

It has been so for hundreds of years.

It all started in the monasteries. Inky-fingered monks sitting hunched in cold cells lit with guttering candles illuminating manuscripts that all looked the same. They told the world what to think and the world thought just as it should.

The monks taught schools and inky-fingered boys sat hunched at desks being told how to act. They in turn told others as they gained the authority of age. Monasteries became churches and churches became offices. Same function though. Tell the world what to think, how to act, what to buy.

In the twenty-first century, the Hegemony continues with its heritage. People still sit hunched. The light comes from neon strips and still gutters. No change. The papers are produced more quickly but have that standard appearance. Still illuminated with images worth a thousand words. Telling people what to buy.

No need any more to tell them what to think, how to act.

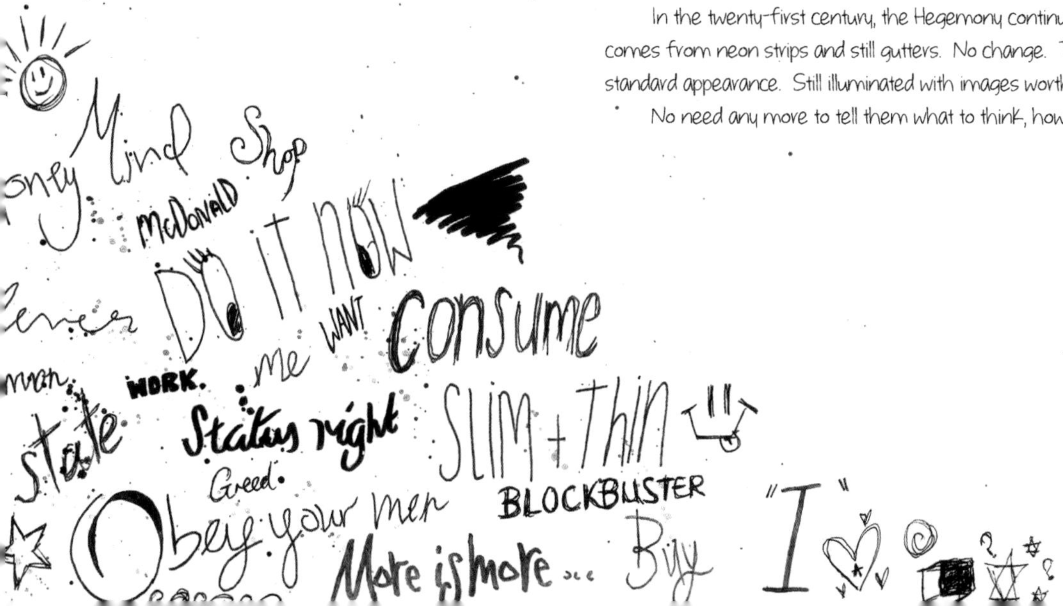

Jail House

I want to tell her I love her, want her ... but I can't.
I want to scream out at her all my anger and hatred ... but I can't.
I want to move, play badminton, snooker, in full control of my limbs ... but I can't.
I want to feel the earth again, crumbling it in my fingers, rolling the pebbles and enjoying their shapes ... but I can't.
I want to smell the flowers, hear the bees, smile at the robin ... but I can't.
I want to enjoy a film on TV or, better still, at the cinema, notice the interesting camera angles, hear the intonations used by good actors ... but I can't.
I want to hear Tom Waites' throaty growl disturb the air, challenge my larynx, charge my imagination ... but I can't.
I want to hear Manchester United fans celebrating yet another win ... but I can't.
I want to spin that tennis ball and enjoy the howl of losing despair coming across the net ... but I can't.
I want to sail my boat, feel movement in the sail and manipulate it to make the best of the wind and waves ... but I can't.
I want to tell her I love her ... but my body is my jail house and I can't.

Kiss

For the first time ever I kissed a woman.

Nothing pre-planned. Not a seduction. Just an urge. Those lips, well, they just had to be kissed.

They felt so soft without the rasp of incipient beard. She was warm too, dry-lipped. My tongue just tip-toed gently over her mouth and stepped tentatively inside. No response.

I raised my arms and touched the back of her head - her glorious autumnal brown hair. This was soft too. It drowned my fingers in its softness and I stroked. And stroked. I could feel these sensations forever if she would let me. I could feel these sensations all over me.

Her arms stayed firmly at her sides. I took heart though because she wasn't pushing me away - just not pulling me in. I started to need more - urgently - and pressed her head closer to mine, moving my tongue, questioning her mouth.

No response.

I gentled, dropped my hand, lifted my head.

And sighed.

She took my hand, gentle too, moved towards the bedroom. Now I hesitated.

The door opened and her husband stepped out, smiled and beckoned. We moved forwards.

Nothing
Much
H

Last Words

I think my epitaph might say,

'Nothing much happened to her.'

I have led an ok life with very little of note in it. It has interested me but is unlikely to entertain anyone else.

I was born some forty years ago. My parents died when I was eight. They were dancing on a cliff when they fell off it and were dashed to death on the rocks below. We had been having a picnic together and I watched as they disappeared forever. My aunt took me on then so I was not homeless.

My aunt was the ugliest woman you have ever seen. But I was a child so I did not notice. She brought me up well and unstintingly.

I lost both my feet in a diving accident when I was seventeen. A shark had them. But I got out of the water and my life was saved so no complaints. My arms became strong and they can do wonderful things with artificial limbs these days.

I ran away to a circus after university. I tried out on the tightrope, the trapeze and the lion house but was not able to discover talent in any of these activities and ended up taking the money at the door. I met my husband-to-be in this way and we were married and happy.

We had two children but they were both killed when our plane crashed coming home from a holiday on the Isle of Wight. Our first - and last - holiday together. My husband and I were the only two survivors and I could only be thankful for that. We divorced soon afterwards. He fell in love with my aunt. Yes, that aunt.

So, you see, nothing much has happened to me.

Moonstone

She was tall, thin, pale and stooped a little. Like a crescent moon from the side, I always thought. Her long straight hair was blonde - almost white, in fact - and her lashes and eyebrows practically invisible. Her skin had that translucency about it that makes it seem almost blue. And she dressed in those pale colours too. Silver, silky blouses, pencil thin, grey skirts, pale blue cardigans.

And around her neck, always the necklace of moonstones.

She told me once, in a very rare moment of intimacy - Selena was ever remote, distant - that she had inherited the necklace. It had come down the distaff side of the family and was always left to the one pale girl in the family. There was always one she said. However hale and hearty the father, there was always one to inherit the moonstone.

I think she never took it off. Perhaps she couldn't.

I last saw her at her window early in the morning, looking like a wraith, wearing a white robe. The necklace shone on her neck, reflecting the setting crescent moon. She was gazing at it and I was startled by the hatred in her eyes. Selena was not known for an excess of emotion. I watched as her hand rose slowly to her neck and she tugged violently at the necklace. Then she seemed to sigh and sag and she turned away. I never saw her again.

What was the mystery of that moonstone necklace and the continuous line of pale sad women who had worn it? Do you know?

NOTHING

When I died it was like nothing I had ever felt before. A slow, quiet passing away of sensation.

My feet had been numb for some while but I couldn't walk anyway so I had not fretted about that. My fingertips tingled for a while but that sensation passed too and I could no longer feel the grainy sheets they covered me with. That pleased me too. I had longed for cool silk to swathe my dying body but the NHS didn't run to that.

I could no longer smell. Gone was the odour of the woman in the corner who was shitting herself to death. Gone was the nauseous perfume of that snooty nurse. Gone too was the salty smell of my treacherous husband's spilt sperm. I was happy that I no longer needed to be in the world of aromas if those were the only scents I was offered.

My sight had begun to fail me long ago. Now, I knew shapes and blurred colours but little else. I didn't need to respond to the people who visited my bedside because I didn't recognise them. Or so I whispered to myself.

Because my hearing got more acute. I could hear the hidden sighs of those on duty visits, the ones who wanted to be elsewhere off to their daily routines. I could hear the skittering heartbeat of the medical student who examined me under the searching eye of the senior doctor and hear the incipient stammer in his voice as he answered her questions. I could hear them discussing me outside the door and knew that I only had hours to live.

I could hear the life force draining away from me. It was serenely lovely.

Obesity

It didn't happen that year. The fat draining I mean.

On Kacoppa our bodies have a facility for draining off excess fat. I've always supposed we've evolved that way because we have such cold winters and very hot summers. Around the spring equinox we start to feel a tingling in our feet and know it's time to seek out a conduit. We stand over a drain for about half an hour - tedious but necessary - so, as always, we turn it into a social occasion. Small apertures open in the soles of our feet and the fat drains out. We feel a bit floppy and dizzy for about an hour afterwards but being a stone or two lighter (or even more in some people) is great compensation. We feast afterwards to celebrate the coming of spring. I think many communities do that, don't they?

Of course it means we don't need to stint on the food, ever. We eat what we like because it's never unhealthy for us as it is for you poor people. And we don't have to exercise - although some of us do for pleasure.

Oh, and the fat is used to heat our buildings.

Anyway, as I said, all this fat draining didn't happen that spring and we took our heavy bodies into the summer. And some were grossly heavy. Mine wasn't too bad because I have quite a physically exacting job but you should have seen some of them! Rolls of it! How they coped in the heat I don't know. Even I felt ill most of the summer. Some died.

The whole thing was investigated, of course, but, as we didn't really know much about why or how it all happened in the first place, it wasn't easy to find out what went wrong. Our medical facilities are good but we have no knowledge of obesity-related diseases (in fact I had to go on the universewideweb even to find the term 'obesity' - we don't have a word for it).

And we were colder because fuel supplies were rationed. There was less food about too - probably a good thing but, as I said, we aren't used to being hungry.

We asked ourselves - will our three feet tingle ever again?

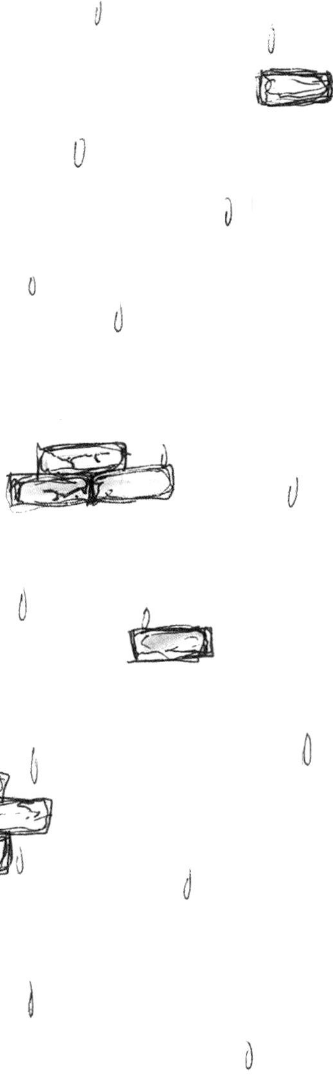

PARTNERS

I sat looking out of the window, idly. It was nearly time to go out and, as always, I was ready early. Les wasn't.

I noticed someone standing on the kerbside down below. He was tall, had a dinky moustache but was otherwise clean-shaven. He smoked a pipe. I thought to myself that I hadn't seen a man smoking a pipe in years.

So, he intrigued me.

He wore a long, grey raincoat, unbuttoned, and carried a man bag. I like men who are confident enough to do that. I noticed that he had a very upright stance too, another plus. I couldn't see the colour of his eyes. I hoped they were grey. His black, shiny hair was swept back across his head in a slightly old-fashioned way - another sign that he was happy to stand out, I thought.

I began to wonder why he was there. Waiting for his girlfriend - or boyfriend - perhaps. Hard to tell. Maybe he was a detective and was watching the house. Bit obvious though. And I didn't think he could be watching our bit of it - couldn't think that anyone would pay to have that happen! Casing the joint! No - he was too old really - but probably lithe enough.

Still, whatever the story, he looked great and I was enjoying watching him.

Until Les came into the room.

'What are you staring at?'

'Just some guy' I said quietly. A frown appeared.

'Let's go Sam - we'll be late.'

I took the outstretched hand and we left.

Queue

She didn't like queues. Who does? But she taught herself to tolerate them. People watched to pass the time.

Today she is queuing for tickets at a station. It's Monday and the queue is slow - people buying their weeklies on cards probably. It's quite a nice day outside - for April. But some people are still dressed for winter - the odd heavy coat, even a scarf. There's someone over her shoulder wearing a balaclava. Now that is overdoing it. Young as well. And, of course, there's the guy wearing sandals and socks. She wonders how come men don't realise how gross this looks. Especially matched with glaringly loud Bermuda shorts like those.

The queue moves forward a pace or two. She looks for the clock. Good, still plenty of time for her train. She's nearly always early. She spots the balaclava again. No, this one's a girl. Odd. Interested now, she cranes her neck to find the other guy. There he is, stalking along beside - yes - another balaclava. Full set! Then she notices that all three are converging, and carrying heavy backpacks. She is slightly alarmed. And now they are simultaneously reaching inside them. Out of the corner of her eye she senses a couple of armed policemen go on the alert.

What's that they're pulling out of the backpacks? She gasps ... it's ...

Tent poles.

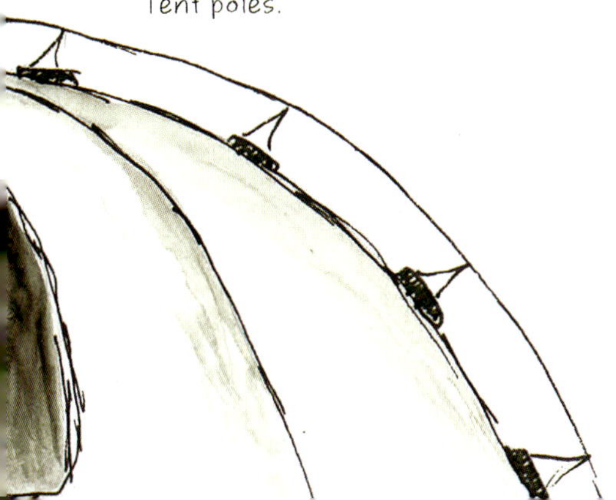

RESTORATION

Welcome back to Kacoppa.

Well, yes, our three feet did tingle again the following spring and we heaved a sigh of relief, drained out loads - and loads - of fat and got on with our lives. Normal service had been restored.

Or had it?

Coincidence or not, after this, all babies hatched on Kacoppa had only two legs. We'd had the occasional baby like this before but never all of them. It was startling and disconcerting to the parents who had laid in the usual set of clothes, none of which now fitted. The babies were examined minutely but nothing else seemed to be wrong with them. As they grew they coped with crawling and walking perfectly well and their balance was excellent. This surprised us. We'd been worried. Our balance on three feet leaves a lot to be desired sometimes!

So many adaptations had to be made for these children. Manufacturers, of course, got on the case quickly - no opportunity lost to make a profit. Furniture was designed to fit the new shapes; nappies, clothes and shoes all came out modelled on two-legged children.

At the age of five the children began fat draining as normal. That was a relief. We had been very careful with their diet up to that point.

When they started school we had to change the curriculum. All our physical exercise is predicated around the possession of three legs so equipment had to be ready for the children. Luckily this was already well thought out as our major athletic competitions challenge people to compete on both three and two legs. These children went straight to the higher-level skills without twitching a foot. We were astonished.

The whole society had to ask itself - how do handicapped people cope so well?

Slug

I thought of him as 'the slug.' (I was never a very nice person.) He was large, very pale and with a suety, damp looking complexion. He spoke ever so slowly and with what I thought of as a country bumpkin accent. So you can see why I felt like that, can't you?

But just beware of stereotypes.

He came into the surgery at the beginning of his night shift and said, slowly,

'Nurse, can you dress the bullet wound in my leg, please?'

Now I pride myself on coping with anything that's thrown at me but this was something else.

'A bullet wound!' I all but shouted. 'How did that happen?'

'Oh' he droned, 'I play cavaliers and roundheads and caught a bullet last time. They're only blanks but they really hurt.'

I was not going to let my image of this man go easily.

'I suppose you're a roundhead?' I said. (I always liked the flamboyant pictures of the cavaliers in our school history books but 'flamboyant' wasn't what was in front of me.)

But you know the answer. Yes - he was a cavalier!

I was forced to let the slug slime away and die.

But in its place I did get a cavalier.

Tranquillity

She sat by the bank of the canal. Life around her was quiet and calm, but busy. The ducks, moor-hens and coots were feeding their young, herding them to safety when they strayed and watching for easy sources of food from passers-by. The water was cool and reflected blue sky and the fresh green and pink of spring blossom above.

She was weary. She'd had a long life and served well. Her body was misshapen now and unreliable. Joints groaned when she moved. Pipes were blocked. She lumbered sluggishly. But she was enjoying this quiet time. The end would not be long coming though.

She heard and felt movement on the bank. Voices sounding sad but determined. She knew it had arrived and tried to be serene. The motor started up, shaking the quietness of the moment and disturbing the waterfowl from their paths.

Gradually she moved away from the bank and out into the middle of the stream.

The narrow-boat 'Tranquillity' was setting out on her final journey.

Upsidedown

A bit of a cliché this, writing about upsidedown upsidedown. Did you think the printer had made a mistake? Did you contemplate taking it back to the bookshop? Did your kindle cope?

Seeing the world upsidedown has been my lot in life. I was born stooped at the waist and those doctors have never been able to straighten me out. For me, upsidedown is rightwayup!

You wonder how I cope, perhaps? How do I eat? Have I ever fucked? Could I have children? What jobs could I do?

Interesting questions - to you. They are not questions I have ever posed. I suppose I did ask myself what jobs I could do but didn't you too? And we all worry about THAT FIRST FUCK don't we? So, sorry, but I am not going to answer your questions. Why should I? You wouldn't ask them of anyone else - well, unless you knew them intimately and we haven't that pleasure.

School was fun. The teachers had no idea how to deal with me and I could do almost anything and get away with it. I passed everything without much work because I'm clever. Even learnt to play the flute. Peeped out between my legs at the concert. It was a hoot seeing the expression on faces when I appeared for my solos and turned my back on them.

Didn't have many friends though.

You'd think I'd get pneumonia wouldn't you, or some sort of gut trouble? But I am very healthy thank you. I like being this way down. It make me different. I stand out in a crowd, though I'm never head and shoulders above everyone else - rather the opposite.

Some problems, of course. Signposts haven't been adapted for me (bloody wheelchair users get everything!) I have to sort of twist and squint upwards. Good thing I've got a great sense of direction and whoever invented satnav has my undying devotion.

And the end of my story will be interesting won't it? I am determined to be buried and just wish I could be there to see the undertaker's face when presented with my body.

You'll enjoy that.

VIOLENCE?

The blood dripped from the ceiling in rich crimson gobbets. It contrasted bleakly with the white and chrome décor. Soaked into the green cloth voraciously.

The half-exsanguinated body lay sprawled on the table. What could be seen of its white flesh gleamed wetly in the harsh lighting. There was a long, red wound down the front of his chest, no longer leaking now he was dead. His eyes were shut but still they seemed to glare accusingly at the people present.

Close to the table stood a guy covered in blood from head to toe. His hands were clenched by his side, holding the knife tightly, and his face held an expression of great dejection and fear. Five other people stood round the table, their faces registering all shades of panic and incredulity. No-one moved or spoke. They all seemed to know this was just the beginning for them of a major, long-drawn out misery. Reactions to the guy's death would have repercussions for all of them.

Violence? What do you think?

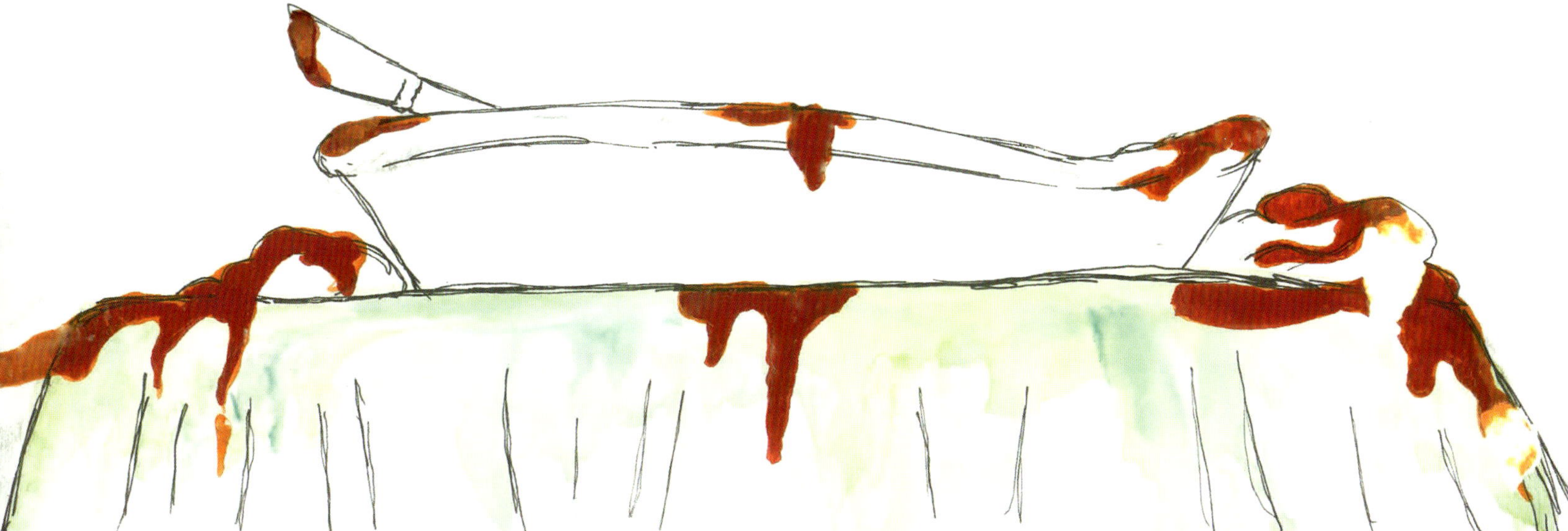

Walnuts

I am a brain surgeon. Always have been I think. From a small child I have liked investigating things, cutting things up, taking them apart. There was never any question that I wouldn't be a doctor and I was single-minded in my career choices so I became a consultant very young.

What is it about brains that fascinate me?

They hide their secrets well in those glistening convoluted folds. When I probed the brain of someone conscious - we can do that you know - they would tell me of forgotten memories I had awoken, snatches of music they heard, smells of childhood long forgotten. But I could never find the right spot again to reproduce those sensations. We still know nothing about how consciousness exists - there seems to be no 'consciousness' centre, no metaphysical knowledge of our own selves.

Yes, it hides its secrets well.

I am a secretive man myself you know. I live alone, have never wanted a companion. My flat is quiet, high above the city here and the most sound it hears is the cracking open of the walnuts I eat every evening for my supper.

Always have.

Xerophytes

We are xerophytes. We have to be. Water barely exists here.

Our memories contain water images. A very long time ago, this place was a swamp. We swam freely in it and, over aeons, crawled out of it, made a living on the land and exploited the water.

We know why we did that. We have a collective memory that contains our race history. We can remember the feuds and the battles. We can recall all those moments of ceremony that we needed in our primitive state to explain our world. We can remember the changes that came upon us microscopically, the sometimes painful adaptations we had to make, the losses we grieved over.

Now we have no need to move. All we need is here.

Now we have no need to talk. We've done all our inane communicating. Chatter, chatter, chatter was all it was. Muddied our waters when they should have been clear. Created misunderstandings - deliberately sometimes. Now the quiet lets us be, has dispelled the old enmities. Our habitat and slow lives give us freedom. We share it freely with the other lives that need to be here. They have some small, insignificant things to give us.

Sometimes you venture close, you humans. But you don't know how to live here. You have inadequate race memories or you might know too. And we can hear how you despise stasis, muteness. Speed is your god now. Chatter is what you do.

Be still and listen.

We can dream and we can remember. And we know. This world is ours and will be long after you are gone.

Be still and listen.

YESTERDAY
30
18
YESTERDAY
YESTERDAY
23
4
YESTERD
11
YESTERDAY
9

Yesterday

Yesterday was a million miles away.
Yesterday changed my world.
Yesterday the sky was blue and the sun shone.
Yesterday I had friends.
Yesterday I was happy and secure.
Yesterday was certainty.
Yesterday I knew who I was.
Yesterday I knew you were in love with me.
Yesterday I thought I was in love with you.
Yesterday I thought I was gay.

ZULU WARRIOR

I asked him what he did and he said he was a Zulu warrior. Yeah, I thought, and I'm the queen's lesbian lover. But I didn't say anything - just drooled.

'Cos he could have been.

He did have a gorgeous body. Even in a dark business suit and white shirt.

I imagined him in one of those feathered skirts they wear. All oiled. Black and shiny and muscled. The drooling spread lower! My imagination went with it. I wondered if the skirt would hide everything. Hoped not! Pictured an erection jutting out between the feathers. That would be something to grab hold of. To feel, fondle. Hard and soft at the same time. Mmmmm!

He looked down at me. I'm not tall and he was well over six feet. He appeared disdainful. I like a dominant man. (Well, in my dreams I do.) His eyes were dark, long thick lashes - but no twinkle. Perhaps being a Zulu warrior beats the humour out of you.

I was a bit flushed and breathing quickly. Could he guess what I was thinking? Hoped not - or did I? My body seemed to be offering an invitation. Would he take it? Did I want him to? Yes ... maybe ... yes ... definitely! I looked up and smiled, lowered my lashes and leaned a little closer.

He put his hand in his pocket and pulled out his business card. Handed it over.

Jon Aikens, Undertaker.

JAN ELLEN

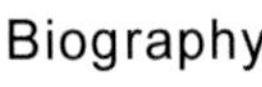

Biography

Jan Ellen brought up two children whilst working in the NHS. Restlessness led her from nursing to training to management; from there to wider education and writing. Her children and three grandchildren enjoy her sense of humour, her frequently changing hair colour and her love of life. From her 7th floor apartment in Sheffield she scans the panoramic horizon to feed her imagination.

THIS BOOK IS DEDICATED TO MY AMAZING CHILDREN - CLARE AND MARK - WHO GIVE ME SO MUCH JOY AND LOVING CARE.

FIZZA AHMED

Biography

Fizza Ahmed is a graduate in BA (hons) Graphic Design from the University of Salford. Amongst designing, she is also currently completing her Level 3 in Childcare and managing a private after school club. When not being driven bonkers by the children or doing all nighters on her design work, Fizza loves to read, drink tons of coffee and window shop for rings.

THIS BOOK IS DEDICATED TO MY SISTERS! FOR ALWAYS SUPPORTING ME AND BEING THERE FOR ME!